100% UNOFFICIAL

ROBLOX
MEGA HITS 3

100%
UNOFFICIAL

First published in Great Britain 2023 by 100% Unofficial,
part of Farshore

An imprint of HarperCollins*Publishers*
1 London Bridge Street, London SE1 9GF
www.farshore.co.uk

HarperCollins*Publishers*
Macken House, 39/40 Mayor Street Upper,
Dublin 1, D01 C9W8, Ireland

Written by Kevin Pettman

This book is an original creation by Farshore
© 2023 HarperCollins*Publishers*

ISBN 978 0 0085 3399 1
Printed in Italy
1

ONLINE SAFETY FOR YOUNGER FANS

Spending time online is great fun! Here are a few simple rules to help younger fans stay safe and
keep the internet a great place to spend time:
- Never give out your real name – don't use it as your username.
- Never give out any of your personal details.
- Never tell anybody which school you go to or how old you are.
- Never tell anybody your password except a parent or a guardian.
- Be aware that you must be 13 or over to create an account on many sites.
Always check the site policy and ask a parent or guardian for permission before registering.
- Always tell a parent or guardian if something is worrying you.
Stay safe online. Any website addresses listed in this book are correct at the time of going to print.
However, Farshore is not responsible for content hosted by third parties. Please be aware that online
content can be subject to change and websites can contain content that is unsuitable for children.
We advise that all children are supervised when using the internet.

Stay safe online. Farshore is not responsible for content hosted by third parties.

ROBLOX
MEGA HITS 3

CONTENTS

WELCOME TO ROBLOX! 7

BLOX FRUITS 8

FLEE THE FACILITY 12

NATURAL DISASTER SURVIVAL 16

BUILD A BOAT FOR TREASURE 20

MAD CITY 24

ALL STAR TOWER DEFENSE 26

BEDWARS 28

HIDE AND SEEK EXTREME 32

PHANTOM FORCES 36

EMERGENCY RESPONSE: LIBERTY COUNTY 40

MY RESTAURANT! 44

DUNGEON QUEST 46

NINJA LEGENDS 50

THE FLOOR IS LAVA 54

SUPER DOOMSPIRE 56

WHAT A ROBLOX RIDE! 60

WELCOME TO ROBLOX!

Nice one – you've entered the greatest gaming experience in the world! In Roblox, you will explore a universe of fantastic games, epic adventures, cool characters, thrilling rewards and so much more. Whether you play on PC, console, tablet or another device, each time you load it up you'll enjoy thrilling fun and great laughs!

Your awesome Roblox Mega Hits 3 book has all you need to get the most out of Roblox's best games. Packed with secrets, strategies, top tips and special info, you'll soon be a leaderboard legend who's showing off your winning moves.

So let the games begin!

BLOX FRUITS

Combat, quests, rewards, boats, exciting missions ... Blox Fruits
has it all and much more! Pick a side and start your adventure
around the islands, earning fruits for increased powers, obtaining
swords and boosting your cash and experience (XP) levels.
Be strong, be brave and good luck!

CREATED BY: GAMER ROBOT INC
YEAR: 2019
GENRE: ADVENTURE

Pick and Play

Do you want to be a powerful pirate or a mega
marine? Choose your side and get your game
face ready! In the safe zone, player versus
player is disabled and you must interact with a
quest giver, accept your first simple instructions
and defeat enemies to raise your level.

Sharp Moves

Keep the cash coming in so that you earn the ability to pick up a sword. With this in hand, those first NPC battles will be no problem! Upgrade to a katana or cutlass and begin to attack your quests like a pro!

Fruit Force

Fruits are essential to your progress. These are not *actual* fruits, but they will grant you the power of the item. You can find them on your travels or buy them from the Blox Fruit dealer, but be warned – they will cost lots of cash and the dealer can run out of stock too!

SHOP

Blox Fruit Dealer

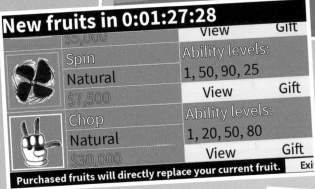

New fruits in 0:01:27:28		
$5,000	View	Gift
Spin	Ability levels:	
Natural	1, 50, 90, 25	
$7,500	View	Gift
Chop	Ability levels:	
Natural	1, 20, 50, 80	
$30,000	View	Gift
Purchased fruits will directly replace your current fruit.		Exit

Healing Health

Keep an eye on your green health bar, which counts down from your max health. You'll take damage during a battle, but your health will generate afterwards. Try to keep your green level maxed so you've always got health.

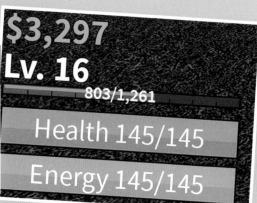

$3,297
Lv. 16
803/1,261
Health 145/145
Energy 145/145

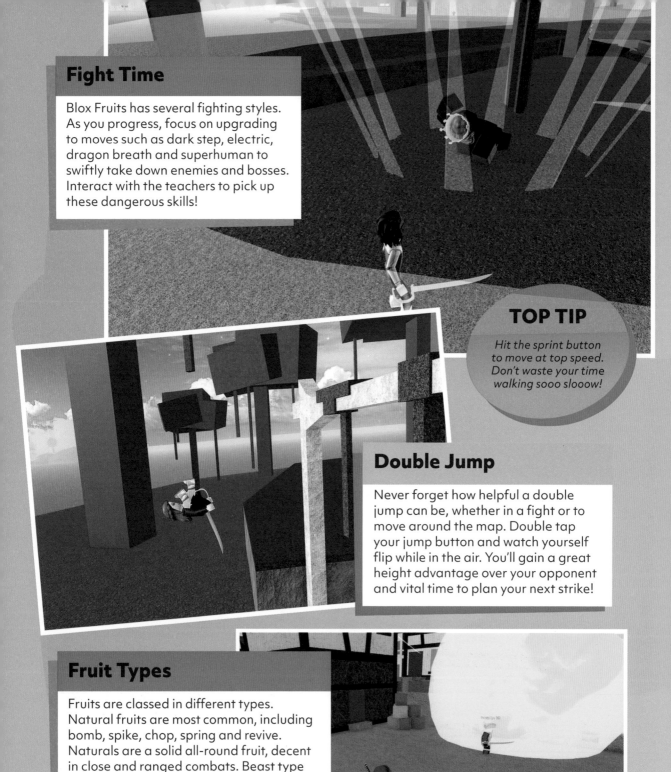

Fight Time

Blox Fruits has several fighting styles. As you progress, focus on upgrading to moves such as dark step, electric, dragon breath and superhuman to swiftly take down enemies and bosses. Interact with the teachers to pick up these dangerous skills!

TOP TIP

Hit the sprint button to move at top speed. Don't waste your time walking sooo slooow!

Double Jump

Never forget how helpful a double jump can be, whether in a fight or to move around the map. Double tap your jump button and watch yourself flip while in the air. You'll gain a great height advantage over your opponent and vital time to plan your next strike!

Fruit Types

Fruits are classed in different types. Natural fruits are most common, including bomb, spike, chop, spring and revive. Naturals are a solid all-round fruit, decent in close and ranged combats. Beast type fruits will transform you into a beast!

Elemental Extras

Start picking up rarer elemental fruits to really boss this game! Flame, for example, is not too expensive and kicks out an impressive knockback and burn damage. Smoke, ice, sand, light and magma are other useful elemental forces to master!

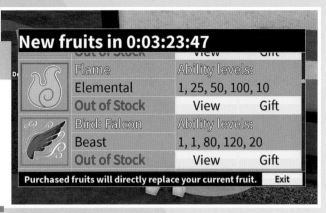

New fruits in 0:03:23:47		
Out of Stock	View	Gift
Flame	Ability levels:	
Elemental	1, 25, 50, 100, 10	
Out of Stock	View	Gift
Bird: Falcon	Ability levels:	
Beast	1, 1, 80, 120, 20	
Out of Stock	View	Gift
Purchased fruits will directly replace your current fruit.		Exit

Bounty and Honor

There is a cool leaderboard system in Blox Fruits. Pirates can scoop up bounty and marines scrap for honour after taking out enemies. To a maximum of 30 million, the level you are currently at will boost your defence or damage ability to a certain percentage.

Spawn Setting

Have you discovered a new island? Make checking the spawn point part of your arrival routine. This means that if you are killed, you'll respawn at a new point and not the previous island you were on. This saves crucial time!

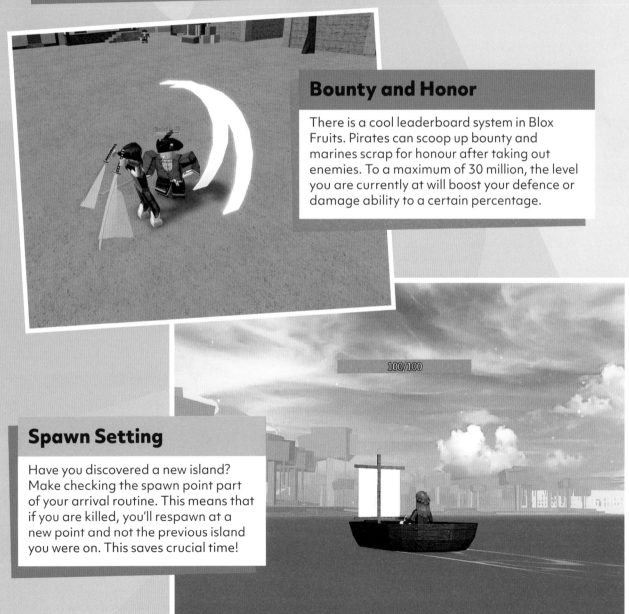

FLEE THE FACILITY

Get ready for a scary (but fun) game of chase as the good guys and the baddies square up! Flee the Facility is mega popular, with billions of visits since 2017. The game attracts all sorts of Robloxians, from horror fans to teams wanting a thrilling adventure. Enjoy!

CREATED BY: **A.W. APPS**
YEAR: **2017**
GENRE: **HORROR**

Five Alive

Five players can join a hectic, horror-packed game of Flee the Facility. Four will be given survivor status, with one unlucky (or lucky!) player designated as the beast. Survivors must hack three to five computers and then escape through one of the two exits to win.

TOP TIP

FTF has a Halloween party in October and November. Join in for limited items, new hammer crates and spooky bundles!

Beast Battle

The beast is out to knock down survivors and trap them in special freezing pods, throwing them in and then watching their health drain away. When their health is totally zapped, that player is eliminated and when all players are wiped out, the beast is victorious!

Rescue Mission

The survivors must work as a team. When one is locked up by the beast, the others can race in to save them. Check the health bars to see who needs rescuing first, but be careful that you don't then become a victim as well!

Credit Rating

When you're successful in hacking machines, rescuing others and – hopefully – fleeing the beast at the end, you're rewarded with credits and XP. These can be traded for more items, but you must first get to level six before you can enter the trading post.

Look Out

One big disadvantage of being the beast is having to be in third-person viewing. This means looking behind isn't easy, allowing survivors to creep around and sneak away when out of the beast's view. Survivors don't have to always be in third-person mode!

Q   Runner

Horror Hearing

When the beast is approaching, listen for the scary sound of its breathing. A sinister soundtrack also kicks in, so keep the music volume up and wear headphones if you can, so that you're extra alert to the predator's presence!

Spectate Mode

Knocked out of a game? Don't just wander around the lobby – why not hit the spectate button to check out the action? You'll pick up tips from others, see how the beast operates and generally have a fun and frightening time as you watch on!

Hack Together

Hacking is a must in Flee the Facility, but as you do it, you become an easy standing target for the beast! Hack together with other survivors and the process will be much quicker, but make sure to always look around the room as you're hacking to check for attacks!

Down Time

It's important to learn how to crouch. As a survivor, this will enable you to drop down and slither away through holes to escape beast attacks. The beast can crouch as well, but it must first drop its hammer.

VIP
- VIP name tag
- VIP badge
- VIP Ban Hammer
- VIP gemstone
- 2x your map vote
- 15% more xp
- 15% more credits

(rejoin game after buying) **BUY NOW**

TOP TIP

Survivors are given a 15-second head start at the beginning, so use the time wisely to track down computers and evade the rampaging beast!

Very Helpful

If you have spare Robux, consider cashing in on a VIP pass. As well as cosmetic upgrades, such as a badge, a cool hammer and a name tag, you'll get a double map vote function and pocket 15 per cent more XP and credits. Very helpful!

Map Changes

Survivors vote which map you play. In 2022, the popular starter map Abandoned Facility was replaced and Forgotten Facility was added. The Airport map is particularly dark and full of twists and turns, so keep playing to know the best routes and moves to make!

NATURAL DISASTER SURVIVAL

Run, shelter, save yourself! Natural Disaster Survival is a tense and exciting adventure of dodging the incoming weather trouble and reaching the next round. It's very simple, but packed with twists, moves and tactics to keep you coming back for more danger!

CREATED BY: **@STICKMASTERLUKE**
YEAR: **2008**
GENRE: **SURVIVAL**

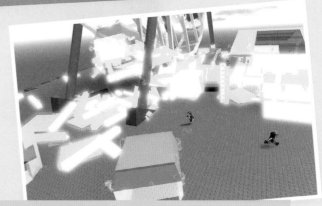

Classic Chaos

One of the oldest Roblox games, it has 'survived' for ages thanks to its fast and frantic gameplay and regular updates! The action begins when you are teleported to a random map and must get ready to face a natural disaster that will sweep through your location. Be prepared!

Weather Warning

You'll face one of many dangerous weather conditions in this game. Before the emergency warning is issued, you'll have a brief spell of time to figure out how to tackle it. Earthquake, sandstorm, fire, acid rain, blizzard and flood are just some examples of what to expect.

Disaster Warning:
Flash Flood! Seek high and stable ground

TOP TIP

Watch out for multi disaster rounds when two disasters are unleashed together. This is mega tough to survive!

Lethal Location

Not only will a random disaster strike, you are also placed in a random map. You can wind up anywhere from a giant glass tower or palace to a racetrack, market or a large school. This makes it tough to find a place to hide and escape the wicked weather.

Ground it Out

Different maps and terrains have good points and bad. For example, the glass tower can give you a high point to escape floods, but it's not very strong, so you could find yourself falling from it if it's hit by a blizzard or acid rain attack. If your health is gone then it's game over!

Screen Alert

The screen will flash a message of what to do – don't be silly and ignore the instruction! If you're told to reach high ground, go inside for protection or brave it in open ground, then just do it. The tactics are simple and time soon runs out for you to reach safety!

TOP TIP

When you die, you spawn in the lobby. From there, you can watch the others wrestle with the danger – it's totally the safest place in NDS!

Mega Meteor

The meteor shower is one of the hardest attacks to survive. You can opt to stay outside, away from buildings, and look closely at the sky to dodge the downwards danger. Or you can go inside, which keeps you away from meteors, but buildings can collapse around you. Eek!

Rumble Route

When an earthquake strikes, get on the open grass and keep clear of any buildings that can collapse and kill you. During a fire, staying in the open grassland is also your number one aim! Jumping around outside will also limit any damage.

Ladder Help

Ladders can often be your best escape route! Look for the ladder at the back of Heights School, leading to the roof. It's ideal in floods and tsunami waves, but remember that incoming water can destroy the building, meaning your lofty hideout is still not safe!

Sky Search

Look at the sky before a disaster is revealed. Can you tell what it will be and make an early dash for cover? A yellow sky means a sandstorm and darkening clouds could signal a thunderstorm, acid rain or a blizzard. Look up for some clever clues!

Health Scare

The deadly virus is a different disaster to all the others. Some players begin with the virus, which then spreads quickly through the map as they cough. Stay out in the open and away from others to last the round. The virus will not cause any damage to buildings and environments.

Brilliant Balloon

Spending Robux on a balloon item can be a real life saver in Natural Disaster Survival! You can jump higher to escape a threat and float safely to the ground if your building collapses. Just make sure you don't float too high – balloons pop at high altitudes!

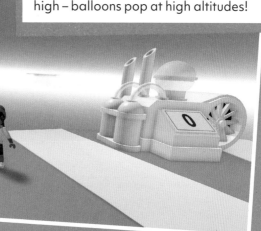

BUILD A BOAT FOR TREASURE

Enjoy building boats? Like to collect treasure? Then Build a Boat for Treasure is the perfect Roblox game for you! Get creative, join a team of boat builders and set sail to tackle stages and avoid obstacles. So, water you waiting for?!

CREATED BY: CHILLZ STUDIOS
YEAR: 2016
GENRE: ADVENTURE

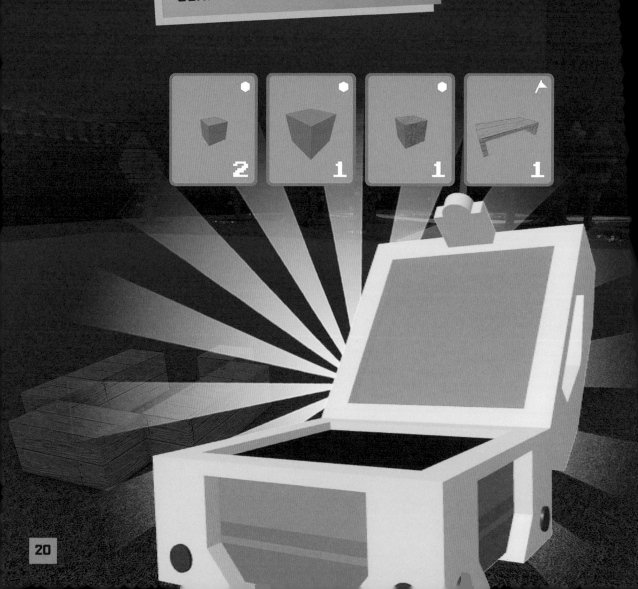

Boat Beginnings

Begin your adventure on the large, flat area beside the water and make this your base for building. Place down a simple boat structure, click the launch button and get yourself out on the waves to begin the quest through the obstacles. This is the simplest way to start an adventure!

Quick Quests

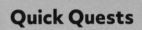

Before you start building, why not open the quests tab and see if you can earn yourself some gold? Quests include target, ramp and dragon. Most beginners start with the soccer quest ... a great way to *kick off*! In this sporty test, just score a goal with the ball and pocket some gold!

TOP TIP

Play in isolation mode to stop players belonging to different teams from entering your boat building area.

Golden Touch

In Build a Boat, gold is the main currency and can be spent on extra chest items in the shop. Some ways to get gold include making progress in your boat, completing quests and winning in PVP mode. Gold can also be used to buy extra save slots.

Block Building

Blocks, also known as parts, are the basis of your builds. Wood blocks are the most common and new players begin with eight of them. Though light, these blocks are no good for strong builds and will suffer more damage on the water than other blocks.

Best Chests

Chests come in common, uncommon, rare, epic and legendary. They range from five gold for common to 405 for the legendary level. Titanium, concrete and obsidian blocks are only found in the top two tier chests, so open one of these and your builds will be seriously boosted!

TOP TIP

When you pass the black wall obstacles on your boat, you pick up gold as a reward. Sail like a pro to keep the treasure racking up!

Awesome Abilities

Ability blocks have special powers. The thruster block gives out thrust force to your construction and the magnet will attract blocks that are within a 4x4 area. Harpoons are perhaps the best of all, shooting a hook that attaches to something and forms a rope. Cool!

Team Play

There are seven teams you can join – white, blue, green, red, black, yellow and magenta. In a team, players work together to build boats faster and to a better design. Each has a team leader, with a crown by their name, and you have the option to switch teams during play!

Stage Set

Boat challenges with obstacles and activities are called stages. Green stages are easiest and red are the most dangerous. The longest stages can be around 300 blocks long. Watch out for secret chests, such as toxic waste, which will need elite skills and focused team work to win!

Game Passes

Creator Chillz Studios hasn't put many passes in this game, but the gold multiplier will double the treasure you collect. It's expensive at 500 Robux, but if you have the Robux for it then you'll soon see your glitzy stash rise to impressive levels!

MAD CITY

Join the police, hero or prisoner team and prepare for a crazy chase through Mad City! The action is constant, with threats coming from every building, street and space in this urban adventure. Finish your missions to make sure your team is on top!

CREATED BY: **SCHWIFTY STUDIOS**
YEAR: **2017**
GENRE: **TOWN AND CITY**

TOP TIP

Wanna speed through the levels? Use hero Hotrod's mega-fast powers and boosted punching ability!

City Chaos

Good or evil? You'll be tracking and catching criminals or out causing trouble around Mad City. Police need to make arrests and defeat the orange-suited baddies. As a prisoner, make sure you rob buildings successfully and loot the coolest items. Look out for the powerful heroes who could stop you!

Super Suits

You need to select which hero to be, suit yourself up and use their special power. An Inferno hero gives off extreme heat and fire, or be the complete opposite and harness Frostbite's extra-cold touch! Get the suit that you think will suit your fighter style best!

Deadly Details

All Mad City roles see players pick up bounty and cash for completing quests and making progress. Rewards can be used to upgrade your weapons and daily challenges are an easy way to increase your levels and XP. Unlock badges too as you boss the city!

Route Planner

As a prisoner, open up your map to get directions to the heist scenes you need to hit. If you're brave enough, pick the pockets of the police to help you escape and crouch or crawl through grounds when the danger level rises. Prisoners need to always be alert or they'll be caught out!

Switch it Up

Fancy a change of role? There's no need to wait until you're eliminated or quit the game. Open your mobile phone, tap the 'change team' option and simply switch sides mid-game. You can go from a prisoner on the run to law-enforcing cop in seconds!

ALL STAR TOWER DEFENSE

All Star Tower Defense (ASTD) is a mega mix of combat, skill, tactics and fun gameplay. With billions of visits since its release and regular updates from Top Down Games to keep gameplay fresh, it's no surprise Robloxians keep coming back for this battle adventure!

CREATED BY: **TOP DOWN GAMES**
YEAR: **2020**
GENRE: **ALL GENRES**

Lv.10

130   Defend

Unit Attack

To kick your tower defence off, you need to equip a unit. Units are the anime-style fighters in ASTD and will rise in levels and power as you succeed in battle. Units are ranked in seconds per attack, range and damage ability, and these characters can be fed and evolved!

Story Mode

ASTD game modes include story, infinite, raids, challenges and trials. Story mode is the most popular for new visitors. Gems, gold and XP are all on offer to victorious players making successful wave defences, as well as all other characters playing.

Summon Up

The summon function allows fighters to recruit primary and secondary characters to help. The system and its connected banner mechanic can look difficult to new players, but you'll soon learn about gem, gold and emerald summoning and how it can raise your status!

TOP TIP

There are over 30 orbs in All Star Tower Defense. Orb items can increase damage and can be won in trials, challenges and raids.

Target Time

Target units at different ranges by adjusting the priority settings of your attack. The priorities include first, last and strong. Select 'strong' to eliminate the most powerful units quickly, or choose 'first' to lock in on the first waves you encounter. Selecting 'closest' deals with enemies right in front of you!

BEDWARS

If you love your bed and believe it's a precious item, then join in with BedWars as you take on enemies that are determined to destroy it! In less than a year this huge Roblox adventure attracted four billion visits, with as many as 100,000 playing at once. That's un-bed-lievable!

CREATED BY: **EASY.GG**
YEAR: **2021**
GENRE: **ALL GENRES**

TOP TIP

BedWars has a server size of 40. This is high for a Roblox game and means your screen will be packed with other players, so get prepped for chaos!

Which War?

From the busy BedWars lobby, choose the game style you'd like to enter. Classic is very popular, but there's also skywars for doubles, ranked for squad play, lucky block for fun and often a selection of epic limited time events. Join the queue and select solo or multi-player options.

Bed Battle

As well as protecting your own bed around the wide variety of BedWars maps, you're also tasked with invading and destroying enemy beds to eliminate players and win. Collecting resources, such as iron, diamonds and emeralds, allows you to upgrade and buy new items.

Kitted Out

BedWars operates with a cool kit system. Kits are fun-looking outfits that have special powers and abilities. Three kits are in the shop for free each week – check out their descriptions to see if you want to take them on. You can also spend Robux to have superior kits!

Kit Tricks

Many of the kits have really helpful abilities as you advance in BedWars. After three eliminations, the Trinity kit offers you a light or a void transformation. Light will heal nearby teammates and void starts zapping energy from opponents. Neat touch, hey?!

29

Rage Up

Keep an eye on your rage meter during melee raids. If you have the Barbarian kit equipped, max out the meter after ten kills and your sword will auto upgrade to the rageblade weapon. This has super 65 damage! Rageblades are also common in lucky block airdrops.

TOP TIP

Toggle the picture mode to get a different view of the action. Don't just stick to the regular first-person camera – keep your eyes peeled for incoming danger!

Pass Master

Soon after joining BedWars, you'll want to experience the Battle Pass system. This function has the free pass and the paid-for route. In free mode there are still several kits, sprays and cosmetic titles to unlock at higher levels. The Battle Pass can also be gifted.

Basic Beginings

With similarities to other blocky games, players spawn with a basic sword and pickaxe. With enough diamonds earned, higher grade armour, blocks, weapons, tools and brewing stands can be obtained. Protect your bed first and play in custom mode for training practice.

Block Build

Get familiar with the types of blocks in BedWars. Surprisingly, a soft block such as wool offers decent protection for your bed, but you'll really want to lay down tougher blocks such as stone, plank and obsidian. Blastproof ceramic will protect beds against TNT blasts!

Give a Gift

Are you in a generous mood, or perhaps have some spare Robux? There's an option to gift a kit to one of your friends in BedWars. That way you can both team up in the same kit and use equal powers and abilities to defend and destroy beds. It's the perfect present!

Extra Events

Keep checking in on BedWars for updates and fun events. Double and triple XP weekends offer a big boost, select skins can be offered for just a short time, new maps are regularly released and exclusive blocks will make appearances. There's no time to sleep in BedWars!

Game On

BedWars developers Easy.gg also make another Roblox game called Islands. You can build your own island, create huge farms and populate them with friendly animals. Just be on high alert for any monsters and bosses that could threaten your island lifestyle!

HIDE AND SEEK EXTREME

Most of us enjoy a simple game of hide and seek ... but this Roblox quest takes that to the EXTREME! This adventure is easy to learn – tiny players just jump in, dash off to hide and hope to stay out of sight once the seeker is released. Good luck and good hiding!

CREATED BY: @TIM7775
YEAR: **2015**
GENRE: **ADVENTURE**

Countdown Scramble

In Hide and Seek Extreme, one random player is selected as the seeker, called 'IT', while all the others are hiders. The hiders have 60 seconds to dash off around the selected map and find a clever hiding spot. When the 60 seconds are up, the seeker is released!

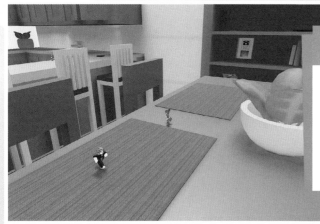

Hide Out

As a hiding player, where will you take cover? Do you go for a high spot and hope that IT doesn't look up and find you? Perhaps staying low on the ground is the sneakiest place to hide? With more experience, you'll soon discover some great getaways from the seeker!

Seeker Skills

The seeker can use one skill against the rest. In a match, this could be the sticky glue spot – if the hiders make contact with it, they will be stuck for a while, allowing IT to charge in and eliminate them. The remote camera is another helpful tool, allowing IT to spy on the scene!

IT

TOP TIP

If you're eliminated, use the time to watch other players on the map. You may discover a great place to hide next time!

>> The Store <<

Location Chase

There are lots of maps to play in. The bedroom has a ladder, bed, TV, furniture, a plant and lots more crafty places to hide. Look for the book near the spawn point as a top-notch, tucked-away place. Sprint around the room to seek a secret location!

Fast Pace

Even when the seeker isn't using a special skill, don't think that you can just out run the chase and avoid being caught! The seeker is slightly faster than the hiders, meaning that in a foot chase across the ground, there's no escape. Stay hidden is the best advice!

Tele Travels

Most maps have a cool teleporter tile. Just jump on this and you'll be whisked away from the scene, popping up in a new spot. It really helps to evade the chasing seeker! Watch out though, because IT can also teleport and remain on your tail!

Spectate Seeker

When you're hiding away in silence, make sure you still keep a very close eye on IT by tapping the spectate button. This allows you to check out exactly where the seeker is and whether you need to move from your hideaway as the chaser comes close!

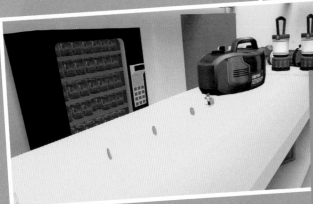

Coin Collect

Around each map are shiny gold coins to collect. Pick these up and spend them in the game store. Buying characters can cost between 200 and 300 credits, and you also pocket ten coins for surviving a round. IT gets five coins for every seeker he finds.

Away Game

The spectate tool shows you where the seeker is, but for a highly accurate reading, look at the 'studs away' information. If this is a high number, such as over 200, then it means you're safe as the seeker isn't nearby. When it tracks down to single numbers, it means IT is closing in!

Stunning Move

Become the scary yeti seeker character and get ready for a ground-breaking special skill! This creature uses a powerful club, which when bashed against the ground sends shockwaves that stun nearby hiders. Awesome! The club has a cooldown time of 13 seconds, though.

TOP TIP

If you pay six Robux, you can choose which hiding room to play in. Otherwise it will be randomly selected just before the countdown begins.

More Chance

Your chances of being selected as IT are low. You can buy the seeker multiplier for 100 Robux and double your selection possibility. The store also has funny pets to equip, cool in-game taunt emoticons and other stuff, such as extra coins and a triple coin converter.

PHANTOM FORCES

If you're accurate with your aim and get a rush from hectic shootouts, then Phantom Forces should definitely be on your Roblox list! It can be a complex and challenging game, but get to grips with it and this first-person shooter is one of the very best in the genre. Load up and roll out ...

CREATED BY: **STYLIS STUDIOS**
YEAR: **2015**
GENRE: **FIRST-PERSON SHOOTER**

TOP TIP

Phantom Forces has loads of fine tuning and setting options. Controller aim acceleration, field of view, toggle sprint and dynamic stance are just some of them!

Group Battle

Phantom Forces sees two teams – the blue-tagged Phantoms and the orange Ghosts – face off around a series of maps. There are game modes, a huge selection of weapons and loadouts and team tactics to master. You need to go all in for this mission!

Take Control

Before heading out on your map, study the control options. Whether you're on console or PC, being able to quickly switch from fire weapon to throw grenade, spot enemy, reloading, crouching, sprinting and more is a must. The power is at your fingertips!

On the Spot

The 'spot enemy' function is ultra helpful. When an opponent is in range, it will mark them with a red dot so that the rest of your team can join in and try to eliminate the player with you. The best way to avoid being spotted is to stay out of sight and try to be super stealthy!

Prime Time

In your primary loadout slot will be machines such as snipers and assault rifles, which are essential for long- and mid-range duels. These often have a high accuracy and will be automatic or semi-automatic firing. Knowing your primary weapons is crucial.

Secondary Slot

Your secondary weapon will usually be a small and easy-to-operate piece of kit, such as a pistol or revolver. While these are lower ranked than rifles, it's a good tip to know how these work, as when the pressure's on, a decent secondary device can be a game changer!

TOP TIP

Pick up your daily login reward each day you open Phantom Forces. It's the easiest way to get items and credits – just click confirm and take what's on offer!

Stat Attack

Don't be too bothered by stats at first, but as you progress you'll eye your rank, XP level, elimination count and other vital readouts. Bigger stats obviously mean you're a more serious Phantom Forces soldier. Unlocking higher-tier weapons will also soon come!

Player			
Rank **122**	Weapon		Reflex Sight
			Muzzle Brake
Health **100**			Stubby Grip
	M16A3		Green Laser
			None

Deal Damage

Where you target an opponent can have an impact on how much damage you deal. Striking an opponent from close-up will pack a punch, but ranged strikes can be less powerful, so you need to be connecting with the prime hit points. You'll soon learn how to cause max damage!

Bursting Out

In understanding game tactics, try to realise the difference between burst firing a weapon or being less heavy on the trigger. Burst firing means you use a lot of ammunition at once for more power, but with less accuracy. Firing less can often increase your aim success!

Scene Change

Phantom Forces is always being updated with new maps. From market towns to castles, deserts, industrial sights, office blocks and warehouses, there will always be obstacles to tackle and vantage points to secure. Choose your mode and make the most of the map!

Game Talk

Get to know some of the language and phrases of the best Phantom Forces operators! 'ADS' means aim down sights, 'CQC' is close-quarters combat, 'nades' refers to grenades and 'vaulting' is a term about an item that's been removed from the game. Top talking tips!

EMERGENCY RESPONSE: LIBERTY COUNTY

Enforce the law, fight fires, maintain the city or break the law – Emergency Response: Liberty County has so much to offer! Select the role you want to take and head off around the city, looking to earn cash, rewards and raise your game status. Welcome to Liberty County!

CREATED BY: POLICE ROLEPLAY COMMUNITY
YEAR: 2018
GENRE: TOWN AND CITY

Work Out

Players begin as decent, law-keeping civilians. There are lots of roles to take in this team, including police and sheriff, firefighter, farmer, hospital worker and restaurant operator. Work hard and pick up your pay checks and XP for following orders and routines!

Crime Scene

Commit a crime as a civilian and the action soon changes – you'll become a wanted villain and the authorities will be out to bring you to justice! Your wanted status is ranked from one to five stars. The good guys will be after you whatever your level!

Bad Moves

The most common crime in Emergency Response: Liberty Country (ER:LC) is robbery. This can be raiding the cash machine, a house, the bank or a jewellery store. Other negative actions are damaging police vehicles and harming other characters. Do these and you'll be chased by the cops!

TOP TIP

As a new player, you get free hair, shirt and trousers to choose for yourself with in the avatar editor.

Take a Tool

Become familiar with the tools of the trade as a criminal. Pick up tools at the store to get your naughty jobs done! A RFID disruptor tool is needed to rob cash machines, house break-ins require a lockpick and pick up a drill if you're brave enough to take down the jewellery store!

Police Profile

All police officers begin at cadet rank, with a basic pistol and cop car. Boost your XP to raise your rank and unlock weapons, equipment and superior pursuit cars. The highest rank is commander at 20,000 XP. Reach this and you'll be an ER:LC law-keeping legend!

Cash In

In ER:LC, you pocket cash for the missions you complete and for staying in the game. Your money can be exchanged for weapons, vehicles, tools and items. Make sure your bank balance is boosted so that the stuff you collect gives you the edge as a good guy or a baddie!

Car Action

Cars, vehicles and helicopters are a big part of this town-and-city platform game! Over 70 types of cars are available, with higher level machines being the coolest, quickest and most expensive! Cars can be customised by entering the vehicle upgrade shop and using your cash.

Combat Skills

With combat mode engaged and a weapon raised, prepare for a crazy time in the city! It's best to use first-person mode for a better aim and take shelter around cars and buildings to protect yourself. Civilians can also use a weapon, but if you commit a crime it's very risky!

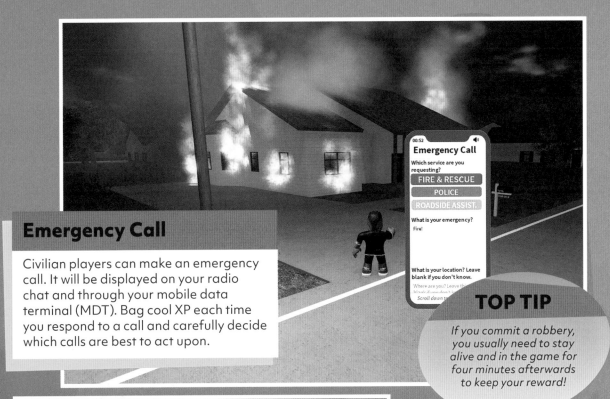

Emergency Call

Civilian players can make an emergency call. It will be displayed on your radio chat and through your mobile data terminal (MDT). Bag cool XP each time you respond to a call and carefully decide which calls are best to act upon.

Emergency Call

Which service are you requesting?

FIRE & RESCUE
POLICE
ROADSIDE ASSIST.

What is your emergency?
Fire!

What is your location? Leave blank if you don't know.

TOP TIP

If you commit a robbery, you usually need to stay alive and in the game for four minutes afterwards to keep your reward!

Mafia Move

A recent ER:LC update added the mafia role. This is an advanced criminal group that works together to take down the county! Any illegal cash raised is shared in the group, but watch out because if one member becomes wanted, all the rest of the gang will be too!

Server Select

ER:LC uses a clever server system. It's ranked in three tiers, with tier 1 for beginners and tier 3 for advanced players. Enter the top tier with 15,000 XP and over 12 hours of game time! This function allows players of equal ability to compete against each other.

MY RESTAURANT!

From the makers of Pet Simulator X and BIG Paintball, this town- and city-Simulator crossover game is weirdly fun. The main task is very simple: just create and run your own restaurant, racking up the cash and keeping the customers happy. Feed your need to play!

CREATED BY: BIG GAMES
YEAR: 2019
GENRE: ALL GENRES

Starting Out

It's easy to get started in My Restaurant! Open your restaurant and interact with the customers that line up. Once they are sat down, they'll need their order taken and then you must cook it. Keep the order stand busy, so you can serve and get cash in your till. Tasty stuff!

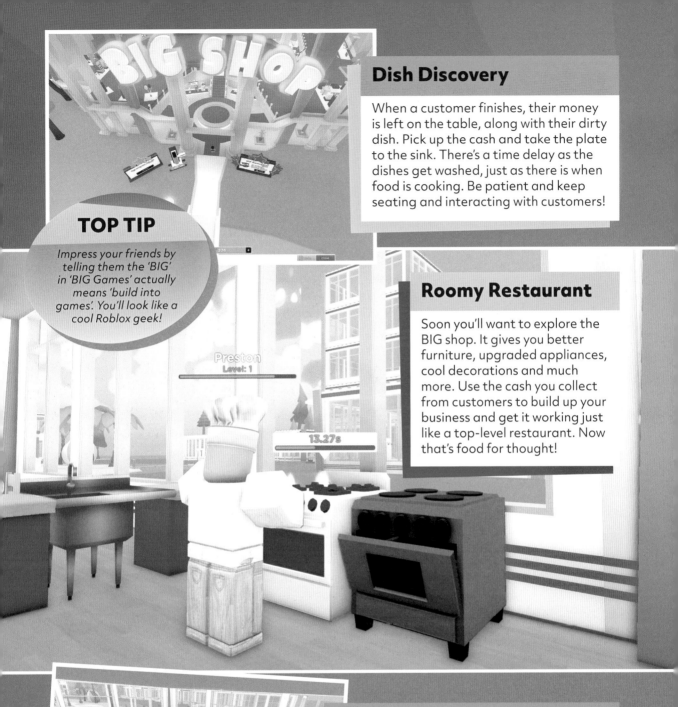

Dish Discovery

When a customer finishes, their money is left on the table, along with their dirty dish. Pick up the cash and take the plate to the sink. There's a time delay as the dishes get washed, just as there is when food is cooking. Be patient and keep seating and interacting with customers!

TOP TIP

Impress your friends by telling them the 'BIG' in 'BIG Games' actually means 'build into games'. You'll look like a cool Roblox geek!

Roomy Restaurant

Soon you'll want to explore the BIG shop. It gives you better furniture, upgraded appliances, cool decorations and much more. Use the cash you collect from customers to build up your business and get it working just like a top-level restaurant. Now that's food for thought!

Hired Help

With your earnings, you must staff your restaurant with waiters and cooks. They are expensive, but the investment is worth it because you won't have to do all the cooking and cleaning yourself. Stoves and sinks soon get busy, so bring in the extra help you'll need!

DUNGEON QUEST

Dungeon Quest is so good, it won an official Bloxy Award from Roblox! If you enjoy action, fighting and upgrading weapons and abilities, then check out this multi-billion game and get your combat skills tested. Can you accept and complete the quest?!

CREATED BY: @VCAFFY
YEAR: 2018
GENRE: ALL GENRES

39   917/917

TOP TIP

Use the practice targets in the lobby to test your weapon skills. Whatever level you are, this will boost how well you can fight!

Dungeon Despair

There are loads of dungeons to explore and conquer. In each dungeon level, waves of mobs will attack you and quickly drain your health. Use your weapons and armour to defeat them, clear the dungeon and progress through the game. Easy to do? No way!

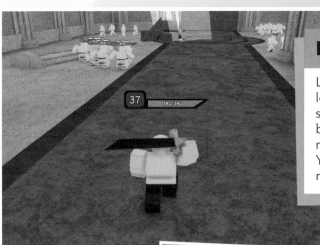

Difficult Decision

Luckily, Dungeon Quest has difficultly levels, so new players can adjust their status and make good progress, even as a beginner. Easy, medium, hard, insane and nightmare are the range of difficulties. You need proper combat powers to beat mobs at the top end of these!

Desert Temple

Desert Temple is the opening dungeon. Here, the sand peasant mobs are your enemy, attacking in frightening groups and quickly gaining ground on you. They fight when approached, but only have 30 HP and deal just 5 to 7 damage per hit in the easy setting.

Boss It

Once you've mastered the dungeon mobs, prepare to battle a boss in each dungeon! After bashing the sand peasants in Desert Temple, the sand giant enters the action. Sand giant boasts 275 HP on easy level and will inflict fire line and smash raids to win a fight!

Player Power

Dungeon Quest can be a solo or squad game. If two players tackle a dungeon, the bad news is that mob powers rise by 30 per cent. If three are playing, it goes up to 60 per cent! Use your extra players to hunt mobs and bosses in packs and to protect each other.

TOP TIP

Dungeon Quest has a helpful data restore button. If you crash or disconnect and drop important stuff, use this to hopefully help bring it back!

Golden Glory

Dungeon Quest's in-game currency is gold. This is pocketed by defeating mobs and bosses to complete a dungeon, or by selling items and collecting your daily rewards. Gold is needed to upgrade your items, which will give more power to your player.

Epic Abilities

As well as melee (close) and ranged (far away) weapon moves, players also have abilities to beat the opposition. Spinning at high speed in a whirlwind will make sure that everything around you is hit and takes damage. This is effective and impressive to see in action!

Armour Up

Mage, warrior and guardian armour are the levels of protection you can equip in Dungeon Quest. These come in a range of sets, such as novice, mercenary and red knight. The greater the rarity and base power, the better the gear's defence!

Cosmetic Calls

If you're flush with Dungeon Quest gold or Robux, adding cosmetic items gives you a superior look in the game, even if they give no actual boost to your performance. Weapons, armour, enchants and titles are on offer as cosmetics. Equip them to give your player a unique look!

Survival Stats

In a battle against mobs and bosses, watch out for your readings related to damage done, healing done and damage taken. Experienced questers will see big numbers in damage done to opponents! Direct stamina, physical power and spell power boost are other stats to watch.

Battle Bonus

Pick up other clever ways to get ahead in this all-action Roblox adventure. Get a game pass to access VIP cosmetics and 20 per cent more XP, or a double gold activator and the ability to have an extra item dropped at the end of each dungeon. Each little gain stacks up for bigger wins!

NINJA LEGENDS

Train your ninja and take on battles to become the mightiest martial art master! Ninja Legends offers plenty of action, but it's not a non-stop fight fest and there's plenty of time to explore islands and the lobby to develop your character. Let the contest begin ...

CREATED BY: **SCRIPTBLOXIAN STUDIOS**
YEAR: **2019**
GENRE: **FIGHTING**

Safe Time

Leave the safe zone in the lobby to kick off your ninja experience. You'll spot the zones to shop, boost skills, sell and trade, and to enter the islands. The clock counts down to duel time, but just tap 'no' if you're not ready to take on a ninja battle yet!

Parkour Perfect

The art of parkour is vital in Ninja Legends. In the lobby you can practise jumping around, landing on treetops and buildings, and becoming familiar with the athletic abilities needed. A ninja must be a master of weapons and combat, but also fearless when moving!

TOP TIP

To double jump while in the air, press space bar (PC), the jump button again (mobile) or the A button (Xbox).

Eternal Island

Lift Off

Looking for an aerial boost? Head to a coloured jump pad, stand on it and see the ninja world from a new angle! These pads are very helpful in getting you up in the air. Seeing what's in the sky is just as important as the obstacles and events around you on the ground.

Double Jumps: 0/1

Double Delight

To really be able to reach the heights in Ninja Legends, the double jump facility is a must-do move! It's so simple, but using it takes your ninja to new heights and areas that a single jump won't achieve. You're not flying, but it feels very close to it!

Secret Stash

While you're jumping around, have your ninja eyes peeled for items that will give you boosts. As an early-game reward, the golden chest is a quality find as it rewards you with 1,000 chi. Make some perfect lands and double jump your way to a secret stash!

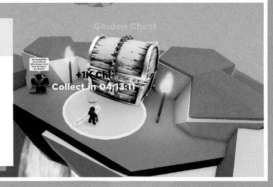

Collect Chi

Chi is one of the main currencies in Ninja Legends. Look for the black-and-white circle in chests and training areas. Use your chi stash to help buy pets and shurikens (weapons and tools). Coins and gems are two other types of currencies to look out for.

Cool King

Want to be the King of the Hill? In the valley training area, jump up to reach this spot and watch your ninja do some relaxing meditation moves. As you chill out, see your chi stash slowly rise. A great way to cash in by doing nothing at all!

Know Ninjitsu

When ninjas unleash fighting moves, both in real fights and training, ninjitsu points are gained. The level of ninjitsu collected depends on the type of sword – which is your primary weapon – you are swinging. Upgrade your sword as soon as you have the required cash!

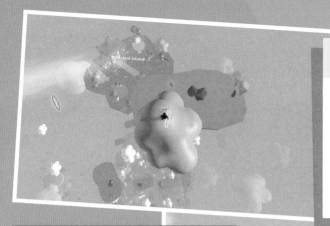

Rank Up

Ninja Legends boasts more than 50 ranks. You begin at basic rookie rank, hoping to soon progress to grasshopper, apprentice, samurai, assassin and further. Superior ranks include dragon evolution, shadow chaos and infinity. Higher fighters win more ninjitsu and coins.

Epic Elements

When you've reached the master rank, you can enter the altar of elements and climb the elements system. These are in-game bonuses that boost things such as pets, chi, shurikens and karma. Blazing entity was added in 2022 – unlock this and you'll really rock!

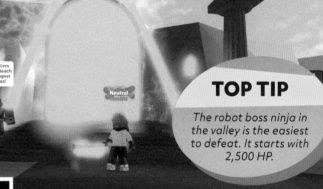

Altar Of Elements
Requires 'Master Of Elements'+ Rank

TOP TIP

The robot boss ninja in the valley is the easiest to defeat. It starts with 2,500 HP.

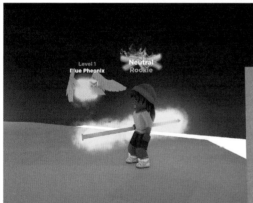

Pet Party

A big part of Ninja Legends is the ability to have pets. It's a complex system, but they can be earned through unlocking crystals, getting packs and by trading. These small companion creatures are fun on-screen and offer important multiplier boosts.

Second Chance

Do you really like Ninja Legends? Well, give Ninja Legends 2 a visit as well! Also made by Scriptbloxian Studios and released in 2020, it has quests, shards and turret systems to get the hang of. Split your time between this and the original game for a great ninja experience!

THE FLOOR IS LAVA

Prepare for some hot Roblox adventures in The Floor is Lava!
As the name suggests, it's a frantic dash as the floor around you fills
with lethal lava. Only the quickest players and the best climbers will
escape the frightening flow of molten liquid!

CREATED BY: **@THELEGENDOFPYRO**
YEAR: **2017**
GENRE: **ADVENTURE**

Chaotic Climb

A game begins by spawning in a random map
with a bunch of other Robloxians. You'll have
just a few seconds to scan the scene, spot
where you can climb and jump to it as the
horrid lava begins to fill the area. Avoid it and
stay in the game until the clock runs down!

Obby Challenge

Treat this game just like an obstacle course. There's really no time for error, or making bad jumps and going in the wrong direction. If you fall from a hill or a tower, it will probably be game over as there's no time to recover the ground. Make the right moves!

Lobby Lessons

From the lobby area, you can go to the viewing platform to watch the current game unfold. You can pick up tips on where to jump, see other players' tactics and where lava can do damage. Copying others is a clever way to progress, and all from the safety of the lobby!

TOP TIP

You can stand on the heads of other players to help you reach the highest spot available.

Robux Reward

The Floor is Lava is one game where having Robux to spend is a real lifesaver! The ultra coil item gives you gravity and speed perks, the grapple hook whisks you to safety and the double jump tool is simple but effective. You can still win without these, but having them helps!

SUPER DOOMSPIRE

With a mix of team tussles and classic search-and-destroy tactics, Super Doomspire rates as one of the best games on Roblox. It's easy to pick up, so whether you're a new player or a seasoned pro, join in for a fun blast of fighting and tower bashing!

CREATED BY: **DOOMSQUIRES**
YEAR: **2019**
GENRE: **FIGHTING**

Spawn Shots

Load up Super Doomspire and when you enter your map, you're charged with wiping out enemy spawns and blowing up their spires. Tactics vary depending on the mode selected, but you'll always be under pressure to hit targets ... or risk being hit and eliminated yourself!

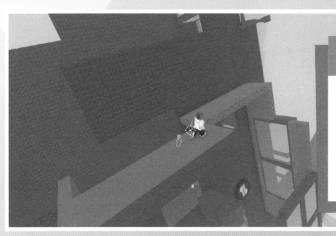

Classic Action

The game's developers call it a free-for-all fight. In classic mode, there are four teams (red, yellow, blue and green) and each is out to destroy others' tower structures. You have weapons to do this and shots can be fired from range or close-up. Think and fight fast!

TOP TIP

The rare brickbreaker sword is a powerful way to damage opponents' buildings.

Infected Fun

Another game mode is called infection. Green infected players take on the red survivors, and action can happen in the dark jungle, storm hill, crimson courtyard or possum city map. Infected teams try to wipe out the survivors before time runs out. The action is infectious!

Knockout Blow

If you are knocked out (KO'd) then it's game over in Super Doomspire! Watch out for defeated players dropping their bricks, which others can then pick up. Bricks are earned by destroying structures and are needed to build new ones.

Bomb Jumping

Bomb jumping is one of the best ways to move around a Super Doomspire map and inflict harm and surprise attacks. It's done by carefully using a bomb to launch yourself in the air. It requires practice, but nail this and your battle success will definitely fly high!

Sword Soar

As well as bomb jumping, players who can swipe their sword while in mid-air will get a game boost. You will also perform a spin, which keeps you up for even longer. This is a great fighting tactic, so use it as much as possible.

Rocket Power

The rocket weapon looks mighty and dangerous, but there are some facts to know when using it. The rocket is a low-impact explosive that should only be used to make safe attacks from a distance. It's accurate, though, and hits the spot when aimed correctly!

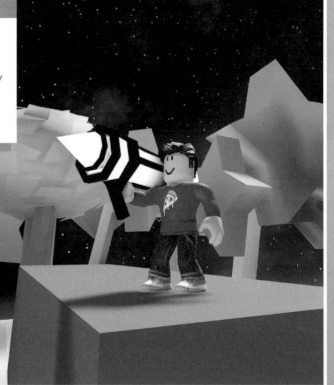

TOP TIP

New items appear in the shop each day. Use your in-game cash to buy some of this gear!

High Impact

Bombs create a powerful explosion and confusion among enemy players. A bomb's special attack makes it stick to the ground, but doing this will reduce its explosiveness by 20 per cent. Use it against buildings and players for maximum damage.

Super Stuff

Another classic weapon is the superball explosive. Like rockets, these are deployed from a distance and can deal 30 damage. It can cause a 'stagger' hit to a team and knock them over. Holding down the fire button ramps up its speed!

Quick Wins

Want some quick tips for Doomspire glory? Aim for the base of a tower to topple it faster. Be aware of the reload time when using a rocket. The lunge sword attack sees you dash forward. Finally, having a lava ball with sword as a primary and secondary weapon combo is a top mix!

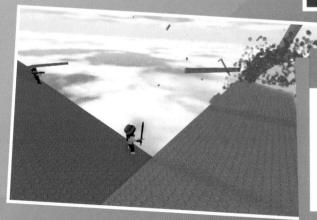

Battle Idea

Super Doomspire is named after another classic Roblox game called Doomspire Brickbattle. Check out this 2017 game for a different take on getting rid of enemy spawns until you're the last team standing. Knowing how to do bomb jumps and rocket jumps is a skill worth having here!

WHAT A ROBLOX RIDE!

Wow – that was an awesome adventure through some of the best Roblox games! Your avatar has seen some epic action, amazing battles, funny scenes ... and there's still loads more to explore! Every time you join in and tap the buttons on screen, there are new Roblox games to enter and new worlds to engage with. That's why it's the best game in the universe.

In Roblox, your journey never ends. Have a blast as you battle in squads with friends or take on automated enemies as a solo star. The action is endless and with constant updates and new quests, there's always something to get your gaming brain buzzing!

Keep on playing and have fun!

61

YOUNGER FANS' GUIDE TO ROBLOX

Roblox might be your first experience of digital socializing, so here are a few simple rules to help you stay safe and keep the internet a great place to spend time.

■ Never give out your real name – don't use it as your username.

■ Never give out any of your personal details.

■ Never tell anybody which school you go to or how old you are.

■ Never tell anybody your password except a parent or guardian.

■ Always tell a parent or guardian if something is worrying you.

Stay safe online. Any website addresses listed in this book are correct at the time of going to print. However, Farshore is not responsible for content hosted by third parties. Please be aware that online content can be subject to change and websites can contain content that is unsuitable for children.
We advise that all children are supervised when using the internet.

PARENTS' GUIDE TO ROBLOX

Roblox has security and privacy settings that enable you to monitor and limit your child's access to the social features on Roblox, or turn them off completely. You can also limit the range of games your child can access, view their activity histories and report inappropriate activity on the site.

To restrict your child from playing, chatting and messaging with others on Roblox, log in to your child's account and click on the gear icon in the upper right-hand corner and select Settings. From here you can access the Security and Privacy menus:

■ Users register for Roblox with their date of birth. It's important for children to enter the correct date because Roblox has default security and privacy settings that vary based on a player's age – this can be checked and changed in Settings.

■ To review and restrict your child's social settings go to Settings and select Privacy. Review the options under Contact Settings and Other Settings. Select No one or Everyone. Note: players age 13 and older have additional options.

■ To control the safety features that are implemented on your child's account, you'll need to set up a 4-digit PIN. This will lock all of the settings, only enabling changes once the PIN is entered. To enable an Account PIN, go to the Settings page, select Security and turn Account PIN to ON.

To help monitor your child's account, you can view the history for certain activities:

■ To view your child's private message history, choose Messages from the menu bar down the left-hand side of the main screen. If the menu bar isn't visible, click on the list icon in the left-hand corner.

■ To view your child's chat history, open the Chat & Party window, located bottom-right. You can then click on any of the listed users to open a window with the chat history.

■ To view your child's online friends and followers, choose Friends from the menu bar down the left-hand side of the main screen.

■ To view your child's creations, choose Develop from the tabs running along the top of the main screen.

■ To view any virtual items purchased and any trade history, choose Trade from the menu bar then go to My Transactions.

While the imagery on Roblox has a largely blocky, digitized look, parents should be aware that some of the user-generated games may include themes or imagery that may be too intense for young or sensitive players:

■ You can limit your child's account to display only a restricted list of available games to play. Go to Settings, select Security and turn on Account Restrictions.

Roblox players of all ages have their posts and chats filtered to prevent personal information being shared, but no filter is foolproof. Roblox asks users and parents to report any inappropriate activity. Check your child's account and look to see if they have friends they do not know. Talk to your child about what to report (including bullying, inappropriate behavior or messages, scams and other game violations):

■ To report concerning behavior on Roblox, use the Report Abuse links located on game, group and user pages and in the Report tab of every game menu.

■ To block another player during a game session, find the user on the leaderboard/player list at the upper-right of the game screen. (If the leaderboard/player list isn't there, open it by clicking on your username in the upper-right corner.) From here, click on the player and select Block User.

For further information, Roblox has created a parents' guide to the website, which can be accessed at https://corp.roblox.com/parents